Playthings

Michelle Birbeck

Dedication

To Pip, for being you.

Playthings

Breathing; loud and heavy in the quiet night. Heart hammering in my chest, beating against my ribs like a bird trying to break free of its cage. But there was no freedom, no chance of escape. It could beat all it likes, as hard as it likes, but my heart was going nowhere. I was going nowhere. Not yet. Not until the time was right.

I had to calm down, to ease away from the excitement running through my veins, begging me to act now. Screw the waiting, I wanted to go, but waiting was essential.

I hate waiting.

It grinds on me so much, eating away a little piece of me every second I have to stay still and silent. For each moment that I pass with waiting, the need rises within me, beating like my heart, begging to be released.

There is no escape for my heart, but there has always been a readily accessible escape for the need. The need that burns bright enough in my soul to eclipse the moon if I leave it untended. It burned now, flaring as hot as fire, knowing that I was about to unleash the beast and all that it brought upon the world.

But not yet.

Not just yet.

First I had to wait. First I had to stalk my prey through the night, watching with eager eyes as it flounced around without a care in the world, preening its feathers like a peacock waiting for a mate. This prey was not so majestic as the peacock, with tail feathers that are sought the world over for their beauty. There were no iridescent purples and greens in the make-up of the whore I watched. Cheap satins and stretched PVC covered her from the waist down, whilst she flashed her wares to passers-by looking for something equally cheap.

I'd never taken a whore before. The prospect of walking up to someone and offering money in exchange for sex was alien to me. I didn't need the money, and I wasn't so desperate that I needed the sex that badly. If I wanted to get laid, I'd go home and take what was offered there. There was always someone waiting for me at home.

There, calm again.

Calm and ready. Eager, even.

My heart was no longer trying to escape through my chest. Instead it was beating steadily, pumping in an even rhythm that was ready for excitement at a moment's notice. Ready for the thrill, for the need to rise up and show my heart what it was really like to want to escape. And what it was like to be given the chance.

Waiting in the shadows, I watched my prey waltz along the streets, not knowing what was waiting for her. Waiting might have been the one part that made my skin itch like I'd slept on poison ivy, but it was also the part that enticed me the most. How these little people could walk around, going about their lives, with no idea I was waiting for them. Not a single clue that I was there, watching their every step in their pathetically normal lives, anticipating what it would be like to bathe in their blood as they gurgled and begged for me to end it.

They all begged for death in the end.

The thought brought a smile to my face, though it wasn't a pleasant one. My kind of smile was the sort that scared small children and made grown men look away in fear. I would wear it all day long, but that meant showing the world what I was. I wasn't ready to let the whole world see what I desired most. Just those with whom I wanted to play, those whose blood would scent my skin with a perfume so subtle only I knew it's presence. The scent would last for days, sometimes weeks, depending on how much time I got to play.

A hand on my shoulder almost made me jump. Almost. The weight and the warmth bleeding through the cold was familiar. Not bothering to turn my attention from the one I wanted, I covered his hand with mine.

"That one," I whispered, my voice breathy with excitement. "I want that one."

I looked up as his gaze followed mine, landing on the whore trotting up and down the street, showing off what she had to offer. His eyes went wide with excitement and approval.

"Good choice." He leaned down, brushing his lips against my cheek for a moment.

He barely even glanced back as he jogged down the street. I watched, waiting yet again. He wouldn't go to the one I wanted first; he'd told me so. I might have been new to taking a whore as my sport of choice, but Darren, he wasn't. He was an old hand at this, even older than I was now.

The first man I killed had been an accident really. I'd always been strange, or so my parents told me, and that led to me hiding what I liked to do better than I perhaps would have. After all, I was a girl, and it wasn't normal for girls to like hunting and blood and feeling the heart of a small bird trapped in my hands, hammering against my skin hard enough to feel like the gentle caress of a feather.

Still, I hadn't meant to start killing people. Then it happened. I'd been walking home, just walking. I hadn't been anywhere special, just a trip to the shop because I fancied some chocolate. I was almost home when it happened. The streetlight was out again, but the darkness never bothered me, not when I had pepper spray in my bag and a knife in my pocket. The man attacked me from behind, stepping out of the dark like a shadow springing to life in a bright light. Screaming hadn't been an option, not with his hand clamped down on my mouth tight enough to bruise. Kicking and scratching seemed like such a waste of time. I couldn't get the angle right and couldn't get any real power behind the blows.

So I reached into my pocket, pulled out the knife and struck.

Such a simple act. Defending myself against an attacker wouldn't have ended badly for me. The police could have come, and it would have been self-defense.

Had I stopped with just one blow.

He'd been so close, though. Close enough to feel the rush of warm breath on my face as my knife knocked the wind out of him. Close enough to feel the blood soak into my jeans, a warm rush flowing steadily over my hand and down my legs.

They're been no one around to stop me. And when the man stopped screaming, the blood seeping away from him whilst I watched, I *played*.

When I first met Darren I was getting drunk in a bar, celebrating my first proper kill. Such a rush of excitement from watching the man's life drain away. I'd slit his throat, but being my first hadn't done it right. The knife went in, and I caught something important, but not important enough. Gurgling and whining, he took almost an hour to die. I sat there, watching, poking around in the open wound, playing in the blood. Oh, how he'd begged! For the ties to be undone. For the pain to stop. For his life to end.

The addition of alcohol to my system even a full day later was enough to have me smiling brightly, sitting happily on cloud nine once more.

I'd started looking at everyone as a potential toy, someone for me to play with and dispose of. Then Darren had looked at me in the bar, and I saw in his eyes what was surely in mine. He looked at me like he wanted to eat me up, spit me out and trample on my corpse until it was nothing but mush.

It should have frightened me. Yet all it did was turn me on.

I think he'd planned on killing me that night.

How things had changed.

The memories made me smile, and I was still ginning wide when a scruffy man approached.

"How much?" he asked in a low voice that was eager and excited.

How in the hell had he mistaken *me* for one of the scantily clad whores just yards away from us. Everything I had to offer was covered in warm clothes ready to weather the evening.

"How much?" he asked again, his voice grating on my nerves.

"I'm not for sale," I spat, clenching my teeth and forcing the words out.

It was tempting to gut the stinking lowlife where he stood, but that would draw attention to myself. Lesson one Darren taught me was to never draw attention to myself. If I wanted to keep playing, to keep feeding that blossoming need in the centre of my chest, then I had to keep getting away with it. I couldn't go gutting someone just yards from a busy street and expect no one to notice.

I ached to.

Standing there in the cold, waiting for Darren to do his thing, staring at the scruffy weakling who'd asked how much I was going for, all I wanted to do was slice him open and feel the heat of his blood running through my fingers. It would have been so nice, too. The initial rush when his flesh split open like a ripe banana dropped on the floor. The gradual slow as the life left his body and there was no more blood for his heart to pump. I wanted it all, and the need rose until it was almost screaming through every inch of me.

So easy. Give him a price. Let him take me somewhere secluded. Take out my knife and slide the sharpened tip into his skin. It was sharp enough that he wouldn't even notice until I hit his sternum and he started struggling to breathe. Sharp knives stopped them screaming so much while they had the chance. By the time they noticed what was happening, they were already drowning in their own blood.

So easy.

So exciting.

So very much what I needed right now.

But not him. No, not him. I already had my sights set on the whore I'd sent Darren after. Something about the way her skin looked under the flickering streetlights made me thirst to see it slick with blood.

"I said, I'm not for sale."

He took my glare at its meaning and shuffled off down the alley, looking for something to sink himself into. Hopefully something full of disease so he'd die a slow and agonising death.

Turning my attention back to the whores, I looked for Darren, but he was already gone. I'd missed part of the show and it made me want to gut the weakling even more. He was so close, and I hated missing any part of the show, even if it was just Darren picking up a whore.

I was left standing in the gathering cold, waiting for the call to say he was ready. The more minutes that passed, the greater my need became.

It wasn't until I'd been stood there for five minutes, counting each and every second as it passed me by, that I realised the man was now stood at the bottom of the alley, watching me with hooded eyes. The look on his face was the all too familiar gaze I'd seen a thousand times before. A cross between hunger and desire, and not the kind of hunger that meant food. It was the kind of hunger that lent itself to deeds done only for money on bodies praying for it to be over so they could get paid and forget it ever happened. The same kind of hunger I'd seen gleaming in Darren's too-dark brown eyes the first time he'd laid eyes on me. I saw it sometimes now, too. After he'd gotten me my choice of victim he'd have his way with them, and then, when he was finished, he'd look at me with that hunger in his eyes. As though he was imagining what it would be like to use me until I died.

He would never find out.

As if on cue my phone chimed in my pocket. Just once, the sound rising through the night like the start of a concert. Slow at first but full of the promise of an unforgettable evening.

The gentle sound brought a smile to my face. It was time.

No reason to answer. No cause to drag the thing from my pocket and see who was calling. Only one person had the number, and only one person rang once and hung up before I could answer. It was safer that way. No calls to trace; easily erasable evidence.

Not that we ever had a problem with evidence. Both of us were careful and cautious.

Turning away from the persistent creature who was determined to get himself killed, I walked down the alley, staying parallel to the main street. Too many whores waiting for a customer out there. In the alley no one would remember me. They were either passed out drunk, busy or too high to give a shit. Nothing but caution and care. Keep your head down, play by the rules, and never, ever run from the police.

Running gave them cause to think you'd done something wrong.

So I kept my head down and I walked. As soon as I was away from sex for hire central I made my way onto the main streets. Hands in my pocket, nothing but pepper spray for protection, and a nice, very good, very expensive fake ID. Just in case.

No sense giving my real name to anyone who happened to stop me on a whim.

The streets were quiet as I walked, following the path we'd already agreed on. I knew where Darren had taken my toy, and though I was heading in the wrong direction half the time, I'd get there in the end.

The list of precautions we took when exercising our... *hobbies* was long and tedious. But a three mile walk to our meeting place was a small price to pay for staying out of jail.

Thoughts of uninterrupted playtime put a smile on my face as the miles bleed away into a memory.

The run down building was a welcome sight after three miles and change. Its derelict exterior rose up to the bitter night, caressing the edges of a starlit sky with the alluring promise of screams and blood.

Perfect.

Despite its rotting doors and broken windows, the air inside felt warm against my skin when I ducked inside. Silence closed around me, making me realise how alive the night had been in the miles between picking my prize and claiming it. Rustling papers and scurrying wildlife faded away, leaving me strangely alone in the quiet.

Keeping me company was the raging need, rushing through me with eagerness and excitement. It filled me just as surely as if I had another person inside my skin, gliding under the surface along with me.

So close to what I wanted. I could almost smell it, *taste* it. Every part of me knew what was coming, and every part of me was gearing up towards it. My muscles tightened with every step, arms aching with the need to have a knife in my hands.

Across the litter strewn floor. Over to the nightmarish stairs. Each step creaked, loud and proud in the darkness. Twisting metal stuck out at the sides, threatening to trip me up and gouge its mark into my flesh. The path to hell was surely paved with such twisting stair cases. Ones that resembled a stack of squished spiders made of dark metal.

Each screech of metal on metal sounded like the screams of the damned, begging to be set free. Begging so fruitlessly for the end to come and the pain to stop. There'd be no end in sight tonight. Not until my need was satisfied with blood and flesh. Not until I decided it was time to die.

Silence fell back around me when I stepped onto the landing. As though those same doomed souls had heard my intentions and wanted no part in my games, so they fell into stillness to avoid my notice.

The need settled along my skin, easing down and waiting in the shadows of my heart.

Just for a little while, I told it. *Not long now.*

Not long indeed. Third door on the left. Half way down the corridor of the old house, concealed in the dark. Those were the instructions Darren had given me.

The door stood open, a soft light trying to force its way into the gloom of the corridor. Red tinted its edges, as though someone had already started the party and I was the last to arrive.

A sinking feeling took up root in my stomach. It was the kind of feeling I'd felt in high school, showing up to a party late. Was I *too* late? Had the prime of the party been and gone, leaving behind nothing more than passed out bodies and piles of washing up?

Of course, I was the strange one in school and rarely got invited to parties, but those I had been to all felt the same. Just like this. Just like everyone was having a joke at my expense and I was the last to know.

Despite Darren's taste at the outer edges of mixing pleasure and pain, he'd never drawn so much blood as to taint the very air with it. Not unless it was his turn to play.

Stalking towards the door, silent as the place would let me, I tried to ignore my need. Tried and failed.

It knew how close I was, how soon until it would be let loose and satisfied in rivers of warm, rushing blood. But when I turned the corner, standing framed in the half dark doorway, the need a screaming desire beating in my chest, my play thing was not the sight that greeted me.

She should have been bound in the middle of the room. Strung up by her arms so her toes were barely scrapping along the floor. Naked and sweaty, breathing hard with fear.

Instead, candles stood in dripping pools of wax, illuminating the room with a soft glow, as though a pair of lovers were making use of the space and time. Their wicks burned brightly, but the darkness pressed in around them, reducing their light to dozens of flickering torches. The red glow made the light dance pink against the walls, a mix of candle light and blood. Peeling wallpaper turned the room into a wilting rose whose petals were clinging to life.

The sight on the floor, however, kept me frozen to the spot. Not the blood or body pieces strewn across a filthy sheet, but the man standing over them, a smile on his face, looking like the cat who got the Christmas turkey. His hands were coated in blood, the stuff dripping from his fingertips and pooling at his feet. It ran in drying streams down his naked body, smeared where he'd enjoyed the feel of it against his skin. The rest of his clothes were no doubt protected in a plastic bag in the corner. Normally the sight would be a pleasurable one... but this was *my* toy.

Debris from a good fucking followed by a fun hour playing in the remains covered the room and his body.

Those were supposed to *my* remains. *Not his.*

I was supposed to be the one covered in blood, panting with excitement at the blood cooling against my skin. *I* was supposed to have felt the life slip away from that body until there was nothing left but skin and bones and blood.

"What did you do?" How level and calm my voice came out. How livid my insides were.

Darren looked at me, and like a child who didn't know what he'd done was wrong, he shrugged. The corners of his mouth lifted in a smirk. "I got carried away."

Carried away? My plaything was in pieces on the floor, bits of flesh scattered around the sheet like discarded toys. She was supposed to be untouched, bound and struggling, scared and waiting to die. Not already dead and dismembered. Ruined!

The need clashed with burning anger. A desire to bathe in death battling with the rising fury of missing the party.

Need dictated that I get down on my knees and play whilst the body was still slightly warm, caress the pieces with my fingertips, relishing the feel of skin on cold skin. It wanted me to take advantage of what I had in front of me, whilst I could.

Anger wanted to rip out Darren's throat. He knew our rules. I picked up his kills and he picked up mine. We never, *ever*, picked up our own. Too many questions if someone was reported missing. Too much suspicion to be seen with them last.

And the need was having far too much fun to be caught and thrown in a cell now.

"She was mine." The faint edge of a growl tinted my words.

"Sorry, sweetie, she was just so… *delectable*." He licked his lips, glancing down at the cooling flesh on the floor. "Why don't you join me? We can still have some fun."

Fun. Yes. I needed fun. Need was winning out over anger, slowly. The blood was there, ready, waiting. *Just let loose*, it whispered, *take what you have. Let me play.*

Then anger and need got together inside me and came up with a perfect solution to placate both. Need wanted blood, any blood, and anger wanted Darren's head on a plate for messing up my sweet, sweet plaything.

Such a simple decision.

I slipped out of my jacket. Darren smiled, and handed me a plastic bag, opening it up wide so I could pile my clothes inside. He watched with eager eyes as I slowly pulled my top over my head. In it went, followed by my bra, dangling from a fingertip, teasing him for a moment.

My jeans were last, and I eased them down my legs, thinking only of how *good* this was going to feel.

Excitement made my breath hitch as Darren offered me a blood soaked hand.

He bent over in front of me and grabbed one of my knives. A twitch of anger vibrated through me. He'd used *my* tools on *my* toy. It was gone by the time he stood up, turned around and handed me the knife, handle first.

I took the knife from him, smiling such a sweet, innocent smile all the while. The weight of it was heavenly against my palm. Strangely, this was where the need receded, taking a back seat so I could enjoy what was to come. It knew that this was it; time to let loose, sit back, and *feel* everything I did as it happened.

In a move I'd practiced so often it was like riding a bike, I drove the blade into Darren's stomach and yanked. It skittered a bit around the breast bone, glancing off and digging into flesh, but settled nicely against his collar bone.

His eyes grew wide, his arms flapping at his sides like a penguin in a panic. A blood covered, soon to be dead penguin. Now the smile on my face was genuine. Sadistic and filled with a sick pleasure, but genuine.

He hadn't seen it coming, and as the blood and guts rushed out of him, spilling over my arm and down my front, chasing away the last of the night's cold air, I leaned forward.

My body brushed his, wet skin against wet skin. I looked him dead in the eye and whispered, "She was *mine*."

He tried to speak, but all that bubbled out of his mouth was air and blood, staining his already blood covered face with a fresh layer of red. Shock filled his eyes at my actions. They were wide, terrified. Once he'd looked at me with eyes intent on devouring me. Now he was just like the rest of them. Scared of dying. Fearful of what came next. Would he live long enough to feel the pain of my blade as it sliced into him, so delicately, cutting bits of his flesh away? Or would he be dead already when the mutilation began?

Darren knew *exactly* what was coming next. He'd watched me play before, with wide eyes full of desire. Not this time.

Anger and need got exactly what they wanted, mingling together with anticipation, making my heart race again, pumping my blood faster and faster. It brought my breath in gasping pants, made me lick my suddenly dry lips over and over.

With a swift yank, I pulled the knife from his chest, stepping back as his body slid to the floor, arm stretched out as if asking why. He landed with a thump, knees first, then face. He was still alive, barely. Soon enough he'd be dead, from blood loss or shock. I'd only nicked his lung really, just enough to make him drown in his own blood whilst he bled to death on the floor.

But he wasn't dead just yet, and I wanted to *play*.

I straddled his back, feeling him squirm under me. Such a waste of the last of his life. Trying to get away was no use. He wouldn't get far.

"You shouldn't have gotten carried away," I told him, tracing bloody patterns out on his back.

Each one bled more than the next, as I dug the knife in deeper and deeper. The flesh split under my blade, blood welling up and spilling over, dripping down his side, mingling with the drying stuff on the floor.

So disappointing that he couldn't scream. I'd cut too deep, leaving him with not enough breath to make my favourite kind of music.

Not even when I began slicing a chunk out of his shoulder, digging into the flesh with the tip of my knife until I hit bone. Then I sliced, gently carving down and down, easing the blade through his skin just as if it was a slab of beef. Except carving beef was never this messy. Blood made the knife slick, slippery against the meat.

It came away from him just as he died. Life left him in a rush of stilled movements and flowing blood. Almost like a cut that just doesn't want to bleed anymore, the blood stilled, Darren stopped trying feebly to fight, and everything in the room fell silent.

I'd never come across a more peaceful time in the whole world. The rush of energy left me as the need settled back down, curling up inside me like a content kitten who just wanted to sleep. The world around me faded away, until everything sounded like I was sat at the bottom of a pool, quiet and insulated.

I could have curled up in the blood and slept the night away quite happily.

Not the best idea, however, to sleep in the middle of a pool of blood, knife in hand, and two bodies cooling on the floor in pieces.

Feeling exceptionally languid, considering how little I'd gotten to play, I rose from the carnage, and padded over to the corner of the room. Settled on the floor were our supplies, limited as they were. Bleach to douse everything with once it was over. One of those camping showers that were so handy for washing off blood, and my clothes, neat and tidy in their bag. No blood there to give away why there was a smile lighting up my face.

As I washed away the slick blood from my skin, smiling all the while, I thought about Darren. Sure, I felt something for him, but it wasn't as though I was in love with him. He was a means to an end, a way to get what I wanted without risking getting caught. I'd done pretty damned well on my own, before having the opportunity to work with someone else. It would be the work of but a moment to go back to hunting on my own.

I'd miss him. He was the only other person I'd met who was just like me. We shared some good times, and some wonderful playthings, but when I said I wanted someone, I was going to have them. No one took *my* toys, least of all Darren.

Once I was sure the blood was gone, I dried off and grabbed the bleach. It was an easy task to spray it over everything, eradicating any trace of me on the bodies. But just in case, given that I knew Darren, and we were personally connected, simple bleach wouldn't do the trick tonight.

There were candles aplenty, flickering in the darkness, still casting their dancing approval over my mess. It would be such a shame to destroy the building, secluded and perfect as it was for my games. But moving the bodies would take time, and I couldn't risk Darren being connected to me. A fire was the perfect way to destroy the evidence of my activities.

So I tipped Darren's clothes out of his bag, and held them over the candles, watching as the flames took hold and greedily ate away at the fabric. By the time anyone noticed the fire, deserted as the area was, it would have taken hold, destroyed any evidence of me, and made it look like something it was and something it wasn't.

Darren caught in the flames after assaulting and butchering the poor whore who'd happened to offer him a price. Maybe she fought back, if they found any evidence of damage to his body. Maybe he did it to himself, twisted mind that he was.

Either way, I walked away from the building before the first flames licked the edge of the night with their greedy hunger for anything that would burn.

There was a smile on my face and a tuneless hum on my lips as I walked the distance back home.

The next morning, all that remained was the ashes of a building, and the unidentified remains of two 'victims.' The fire had done its job, destroying almost everything, so all anyone knew was that a man had been with a woman, and that both had died.

Watching the news, seeing the emergency workers wheeling two body bags from the debris, the need stirred from its slumber, peeking out at the destruction, whispering, 'is it time to play yet?'

Other books by Michelle Birbeck

The Keepers' Chronicles:

The Last Keeper

Last Chance

Exposure (Coming in 2014)

A Glimpse Into Darkness: A Keepers' Chronicles Short Story

Novels:

The Stars Are Falling

Short Horror Stories:

Consequences

Isolation (Free ebook)

Survival Instincts (Free ebook)

The Perfect Gift (Free ebook)

About the author

Michelle has been reading and writing her whole life. Her earliest memory of books was when she was five and decided to try and teach her fish how to read, by putting her Beatrix Potter books *in* the fish tank with them. Since then her love of books has grown, and now she is writing her own and looking forward to seeing them on her shelves, though they won't be going anywhere near the fish tank.

You can find more information on twitter, facebook, and her website:

Facebook.com/MichelleBirbeck

Twitter: @michellebirbeck

www.michellebirbeck.co.uk